Y0-EHY-691

Mom's New Job

Inquiries should be addressed to Raintree Publishers Limited,
205 West Highland Avenue, Milwaukee, Wisconsin 53203.

Library of Congress Number: 77-27982

1 2 3 4 5 6 7 8 9 0 82 81 80 79 78

Printed in the United States of America.

Library of Congress Cataloging in Publication Data

Sawyer, Paul.
Mom's new job.

SUMMARY: Her mother's decision to take a new
job causes anxiety for a young girl.
[1. Mothers — Employment — Fiction] I. Bostrom, Roald.
II. Title.
PZ7.S2685Mo [E] 77-27982
ISBN 0-8172-1150-0 lib. bdg.

Mom's New Job

Words by Paul Sawyer

Pictures by Roald Bostrom

Childrens Press

One night Mary, who was nine years old, had a hard time falling asleep. She climbed out of bed to get a drink of water. On her way to the bathroom, Mary heard her parents talking in the living room.

"Well," Mom was saying to Dad, "what do you think?"

"I think it's a good idea," said Dad.

"Since we both agree," said Mom, "it's settled. I'll start looking for a job tomorrow."

Mary was surprised. ''Mom's getting a job,'' she said to herself. Forgetting about the drink of water, she tiptoed back to her room. She patted Prince, the big dog who slept at the foot of her bed, and slid under the covers. A job, she thought. Mom's getting a job. Why does she want to get a job? What will happen to me? Who will help me get ready for school in the morning? Who will make my breakfast? Who will be waiting for me when I come home in the afternoon?
Who . . . ? Who . . . ?

Mary was still worrying when she fell asleep.

During the next few days Mary wondered whether she would find Mom suddenly gone from the house when she got up or when she came home from school. But Mom was always there. Mary kept hoping that her mother wouldn't find a job.

But on Friday evening, at dinner, it happened.

"Mary," Mom said, "I want to tell you that I've found a job. They want me to start on Monday."

Tears began to form in Mary's eyes. She tried to blink them back but it was no use. Drop after drop flowed down her cheeks.

"Why are you crying, Mary?" Dad asked her.

"What's wrong?" asked Mom.

"Why do you have to get a job, Mom?" Mary cried. "I don't understand. Why don't you want to stay home anymore? Are you mad at me? Are you going to leave me all by myself?"

Mom threw her arms around Mary. "Oh, no, Mary, it's not because of anything you've done."

Then Mom and Dad explained. Little by little Mary came to understand that Dad was earning enough money for the family to live on. But because everything cost more money than it used to, it was important that both her parents work.

Then Dad said, ‘‘Mom will be gone from home all day. Just like you and me. That will be a big change for her. It will be a big change for us too. You have always been a big help to Mom. Now you and I will have to be an even bigger help. We will all have to pitch in and share the cooking and cleaning and other jobs around the house.’’

‘‘I'll be at work when you get home from school,’’ Mom said. ‘‘But you won't be alone. I've asked Mrs. Wilson and Mrs. Adams to keep an eye on you. They will be nearby if you need them. And I'll be getting home shortly after you do.’’

Mary liked Mrs. Wilson and Mrs. Adams. They lived only a few houses away. They were the mothers of her two best friends, Jenny and Grace.

Dad asked her if she felt better about Mom's new job.

"I feel a little better, but I'm still a little scared too," Mary answered.

Then Mom said, "It's natural to feel a little scared of changes. When I start my new job, some things will be new and different for you and Dad and me. But if we all try very hard, maybe those changes won't be so bad after all."

Monday morning was just like every other school morning. Mom got Mary up, laid out her clothes, made a good breakfast, and saw to it that she brushed her teeth. Then Mom gave her a key to the back door. This was something very new and different. Mary had never had a key to the house before. It made her feel important and grown up. She wondered what it would be like when she came home.

All day at school, Mary thought about returning to an empty house. Her fears grew as the school bus stopped at her street.

Mary got off the bus and walked slowly up the street. There was the house. It seemed big and unfriendly. She stood at the back door and put the key in the lock. Suddenly she felt very much alone and afraid. She turned the key, opened the door, and walked in.

The next few minutes were the busiest Mary had ever known. Prince darted up to her, barking joyfully and wagging his tail so fast it looked like a blur. Then she spotted a box of her favorite cookies on the kitchen table. Next to the box was a note. "Have some cookies and a glass of milk. But don't spoil your appetite. The milk is in the refrigerator. Please help me by setting the table for dinner. I'll be home soon. Remember to call Mrs. Wilson or Mrs. Adams if there's any problem. Love, Mom." Mary began to feel a little better.

CHARLESTON RECEIPTS

Just as she sat down to eat, the telephone rang. It was Mom. ''How are you, darling?'' she asked.

''I'm all right, Mom,'' Mary said. ''How are you? How is your new job?'' Before Mom could answer there was a knock on the back door. Mary looked out the window and saw that it was Jenny and Grace. ''Just a minute, Mom,'' Mary said, and she opened the door.

''Are you ready to play with us?'' the girls asked.

''Mom,'' Mary said, ''Jenny and Grace are here to play with me. I'm going to have to say good-bye now. I'll see you later.''

No sooner had Mary hung up than the phone rang again. It was Mrs. Wilson, wanting to know how things were and if she could help Mary in any way. "No, thank you very much," Mary said. "I can manage."

And a minute or two later, when Mrs. Adams called, Mary told her the same thing.

JOY

Mary quickly set the table for dinner. Then she went outside and played with Jenny and Grace. Prince joined in whenever there was something for a big dog to do.

When Mom came home, Mary was sitting in a big chair, reading a story.

"Thank you for setting the table, Mary," Mom said, throwing her arms around her. "My day was so busy! How was your day?"

"My day was busy too, Mom," Mary said happily. "I didn't feel so alone after all."

"I'm very proud of you, Mary," Mom said. "Let's talk while we get dinner started."

Pocket

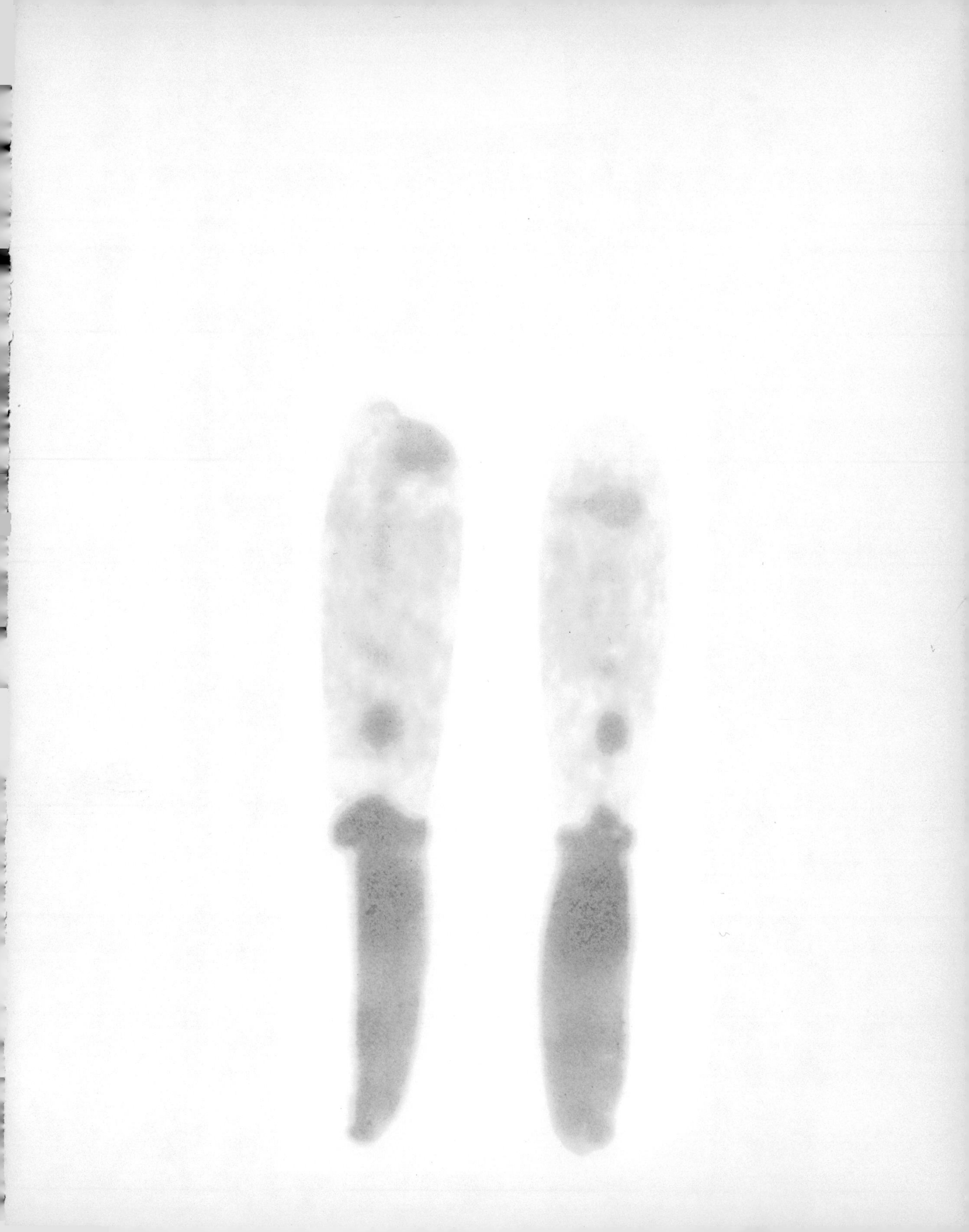

SCHEELE MEMORIAL LIBRARY
3 6655 00031162 1
S271 Mom
Sawyer, Paul./Mom's new job /